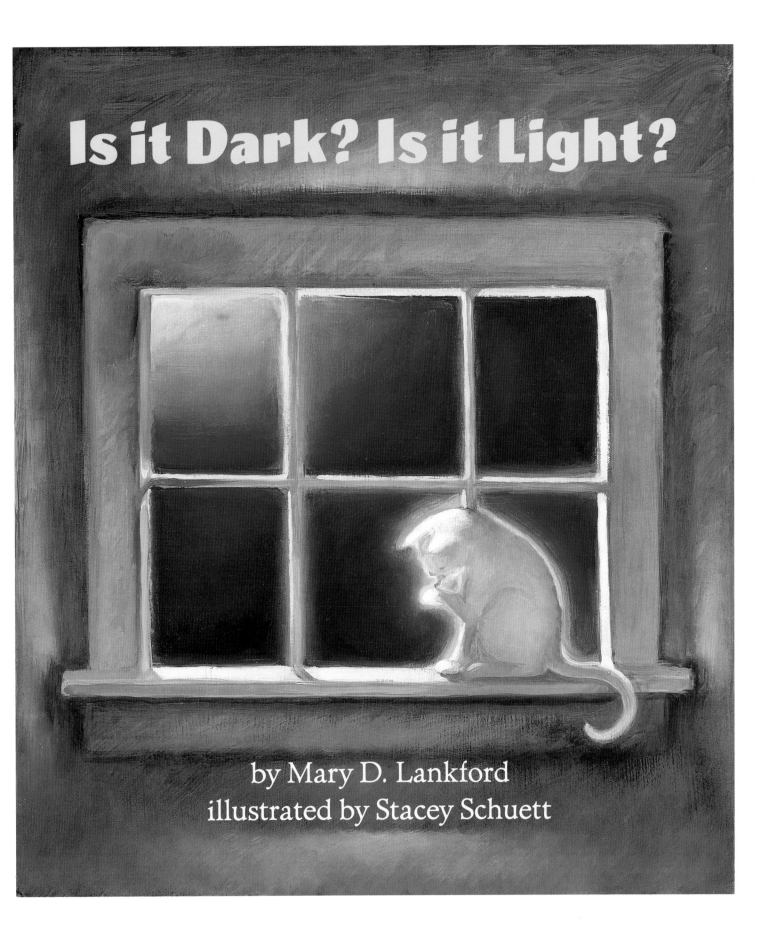

Is it Dark? Is it Light?

by Mary D. Lankford

illustrated by Stacey Schuett

ALFRED A. KNOPF 🐎 NEW YORK

THIS IS A BORZOI BOOK PUBLISHED BY ALFRED A. KNOPF, INC.

Text copyright © 1991 by Mary D. Lankford
Illustrations copyright © 1991 by Stacey Schuett
All rights reserved under International and Pan-American Copyright
Conventions. Published in the United States by Alfred A. Knopf, Inc.,
New York, and simultaneously in Canada by Random House of
Canada Limited, Toronto. Distributed by Random House,
Inc., New York. Manufactured in Singapore.
Book design by Elizabeth Hardie

2 4 6 8 0 9 7 5 3 1

Library of Congress Cataloging-in-Publication Data
Lankford, Mary D. Is it dark? Is it light? / by Mary D. Lankford;
illustrated by Stacey Schuett. p. cm.
Summary: While describing the moon's appearance,
two children introduce pairs of opposites.
ISBN 0-679-81579-1 (trade)—ISBN 0-679-91579-6 (lib. bdg.)
[1. Moon—Fiction. 2. English language
—Synonyms and antonyms—Fiction.]
I. Schuett, Stacey, ill. II. Title.
PZ7.L2773Is 1991 [E]—dc20 90-21492 CIP AC

For my parents, Clifford and Myrtle Balthrop,
who gave me the moon,
and for my children, Lynnette, Bobby, Layne, and Leslie,
who will forever be my moon magic
—M.D.L.

To Mom and Butch
—S.S.

Is it square?   No, it's round.

Is it near?

No, it's far.

Is it little?   No, it's big.

Is it down?   No, it's up.

Is it empty?   No, it's full.

Is it loud?   No, it's quiet.

Is it wet?   No, it's dry.

Is it hot?   No, it's cold.

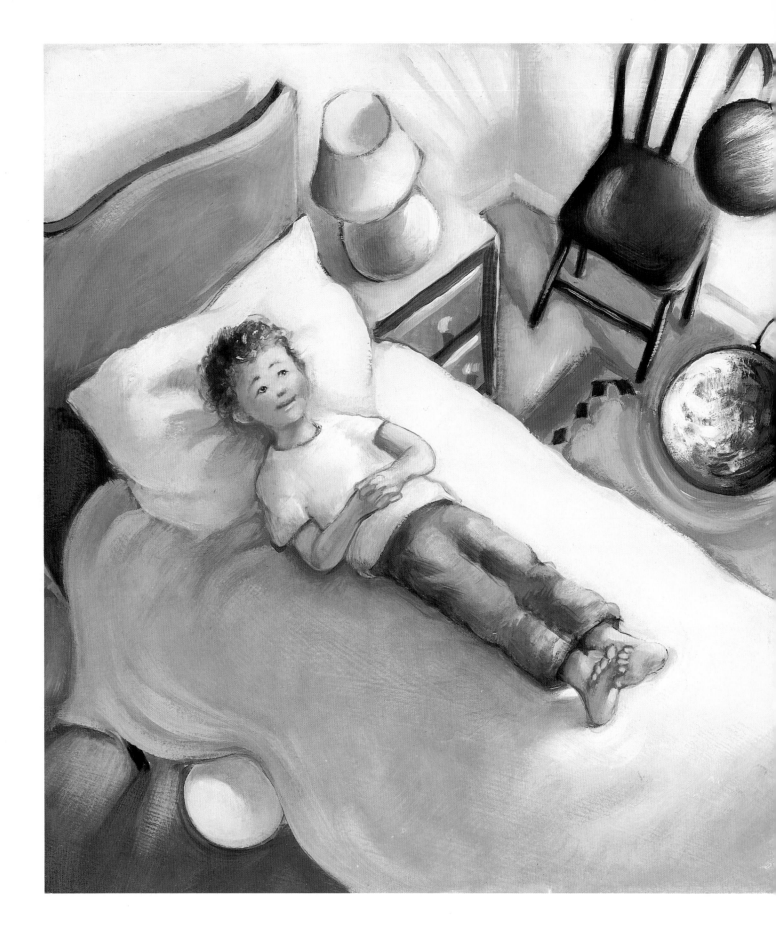

Is it under?

No, it's over.

Is it dark?

No, it's light.

Is it dim?

No, it's bright.

Is it shadow?   No, it's shimmer.

Tell me, please...What is it?

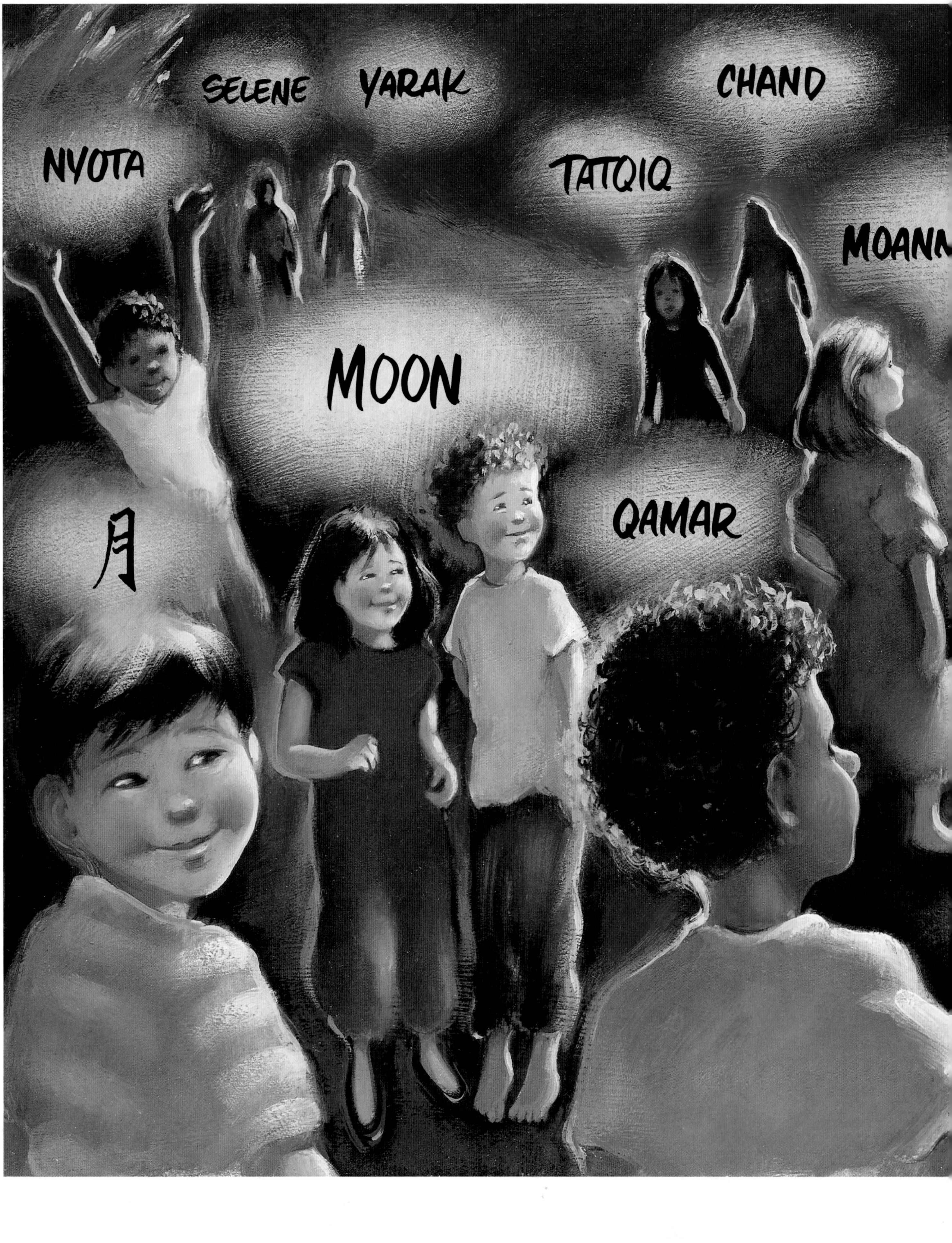

SELENE
YARAK
CHAND
NYOTA
TATQIQ
MOON
月
QAMAR

MAAN

LUNE

MOND

LUNA

луна

The Moon

Arabic	. . . . *qamar*	Hindi	. . . .	*chand*
Chinese	. . . . 月	Italian	. . . .	*luna*
Dutch	. . . . *maan*	Norwegian	. . . . . .	*moanne*
English	. . . . *moon*	Russian	. . . .	лунa
French	. . . . *lune*	Spanish	. . . .	*luna*
German	. . . . *mond*	Swahili	. . . .	*nyota*
Greek	. . . . *selene*	Urdu	. . . .	*chand*
Hebrew	. . . . *yarak*	Uummarmiut	. . . . .	*tatqiq*
		(Native American)		

Mary D. Lankford was born and raised in Denton, Texas. She graduated from the University of North Texas and received a Master of Library Science from Texas Woman's University. She has worked with the Irving Public Schools since 1966 as the director of library and media services. Ms. Lankford has been president of the Texas Library Association and is a regional director on the board of directors of the American Association of School Librarians.

A cloud-covered moon and a granddaughter inspired this book.

Stacey Schuett was born in Elmhurst, Illinois, and studied painting at the University of California at Davis. Her work has appeared in national publications and has been widely exhibited. This is her fourth picture book.

Ms. Schuett lives in Sonoma County, California.